THE ODYSSEY

RETOLD BY PAULINE FRANCIS

Evans

A L I S

2617469

Published by Evans Brothers Limited
2A Portman Mansions
Chiltern Street
London W1U 6NR

© Evans Brothers Limited 2008
First published 2008

Printed in China

British Library Cataloguing in Publication data
Francis, Pauline
   The Odyssey. - (Fast track classics)
   1. Odysseus (Greek mythology) - Juvenile fiction
   2. Adventure stories 3. Children's stories
   I. Title II. Homer
   823.9'2[J]

ISBN-13: 978 0237 53443 1

VISIT OUR WEBSITE

Evans

www.evansbooks.co.uk

THE ODYSSEY

Introduction

The *Odyssey* is a poem of about 12,000 lines. It is thought to have been written by a Greek poet called Homer, towards the end of the eighth century BC. Very little is known about Homer – except that he is said to have been blind. This poem would have been told, or sung, to people who could not read.

The *Odyssey* tells the story of the return of Odysseus – the King of Ithaca – from the Trojan War. In this poem, the home is the centre of the story, rather than the battlefield as it was in the *Iliad.*

When the Greeks had defeated and burned Troy, the Greek leaders led their own ships home. Some reached home quickly and safely, others died on the way. But Odysseus took many years to reach his home in Ithaca – years full of suffering and great danger.

By the time he came home, his son Telemachus was a young man.

Odysseus' journey might have taken even longer, but for the gods. They met to discuss his fate and the disasters that he had faced on his journey – and decided that it was time for him to go home.

But when Odysseus arrived in Ithaca, his problems were not yet over…

Some of the characters in the Odyssey

Gods and Goddesses

Athene daughter of **Zeus**; pro-Greek
Calypso goddess of silence; daughter of the ocean
Cyclops the one-eyed son of **Poseidon**
Circe daughter of a goddess and the sun; an enchantress
Hades brother of **Zeus**; he rules the land of the Dead (the Underworld)
Hermes a messenger of **Zeus**; a guide for the Dead; carries a golden rod
Poseidon younger brother of **Zeus**
Zeus the most powerful of the gods

Greeks

Laertes father of **Odysseus**
Odysseus King of Ithaca; the originator of the wooden horse; favourite of **Athene**
Penelope the wife of **Odysseus**
Telemachus the son of **Odysseus** and **Penelope**

CHAPTER ONE

The Cyclops

When Odysseus and his twelve ships sailed home from the Trojan War, they faced many dangers on the islands where they stopped to find food and water. And at sea, they faced terrible storms.

On the tenth day of their journey, they came to land again. Opposite the harbour was a wooded island, inhabited only by wild goats.

'We shall stay here,' Odysseus commanded, 'until I find out what dangers may await us on the mainland.'

When they had eaten, Odysseus, and twelve of his best men, crossed to the mainland. Here they came to an empty cave, surrounded by a stone wall, which held many lambs. Taking food and wine, they went into the cave. They lit a fire and helped themselves to some of the cheese that they found there.

Towards sunset, they heard the sound of sheep outside. A shadow fell over the entrance to the cave. Odysseus saw a monster, with only one enormous eye in the middle of his forehead, herding his sheep into the cave.

'NO!' Odysseus whispered to his men. 'We have come to the land of the Cyclopes. They are the one-eyed sons of Poseidon, the sea god. They are fierce people who live in mountain caves. They have *no* sense of right or wrong.'

The monster pulled an enormous rock across the entrance to the cave, so that his sheep could not escape. Then he lit a fire and sat down. Suddenly, in the firelight, the Cyclops caught sight of Odysseus and his men.

'Strangers!' he bellowed. 'Who are you?'

'We are Greeks,' Odysseus replied, 'who have been besieging Troy these last nine years. Now we are sailing home, but we have been blown off our course. Good sir, we seek your kindness. Our god is Zeus, and he is the god of guests.'

'Stranger, you must be a fool,' the Cyclops boomed. 'We Cyclopes care *nothing* for the gods – except for our father, Poseidon.'

As he spoke, he picked up two of the men and beat their heads on the ground. Then he tore them to pieces and devoured them, like a mountain lion. The others wept as they watched, and prayed to Zeus.

'There is no point in killing him,' Odysseus said to himself, 'for we shall not be able to move the rock to escape from this terrible place.'

The next morning, the Cyclops ate two more of Odysseus' companions. Then he drove his sheep outside and blocked up the entrance once more. Odysseus, with murder in his heart, had an idea. The Cyclops had left behind his wooden stick, as tall as a ship's mast.

'Sharpen the end!' he commanded his men, 'and hide it!'

That evening, when the Cyclops came back with his flock once more, he snatched up two men for his evening meal. Odysseus offered him wine to wash down their flesh.

'What is your name?' the Cyclops asked Odysseus.

'Nobody,' Odysseus replied, offering him more wine.

The Cyclops drank until he toppled to the ground, asleep.

At once, Odysseus thrust the enormous stick into the fire and, when it was hot, he hammered it into the Cyclops' eye. It hissed like hot metal does when a smith plunges it into cold water. The Cyclops woke up, uttered a terrible shriek and pulled out the stake. Other Cyclopes living nearby came to see what was wrong.

'Polyphemus!' they called. 'Why do you spoil our sleep with all this noise?'

'Nobody is killing me!' he cried.

'Then you are a fool,' they laughed.

The blind Cyclops, moaning with pain, pushed the rock from the mouth of the cave, and sat across the entrance.

'Now I'll catch them as they leave my cave!' he thought.

Another plan formed in Odysseus' head. He commanded his men to lash the sheep together – three at a time – with willow branches from the giant's bed. Each man tied himself under the belly of the middle sheep. In this way, they all were able to escape from the cave. They ran to their boat and set sail for the island. The Cyclops was so angry that he hurled a rock at them and almost washed them back to the mainland.

'Cyclops!' Odysseus shouted. 'If anyone ever asks how you came to be blind, tell them you were blinded by Odysseus.'

Reaching the island again, they sacrificed to Zeus the big ram that had carried Odysseus from the cave. And when dawn appeared, they sailed on.

They left that island with heavy hearts, grieving for the dear friends they had lost, but glad at their own escape from death.

As they came close to Ithaca, their ships were blown by strong winds to another island full of tall men who hurled rocks down onto them. And out of the twelve ships, only one was left.

'Poseidon has answered the prayer of his son, the Cyclops,' Odysseus wept.

CHAPTER TWO

A Wicked Enchantress

Odysseus and his surviving men came to another island. Silently, they brought their ship into harbour. Then, exhausted, they rested on the beach for two days.

At dawn, on the third day, Odysseus took his spear and sword and left the ship. He climbed to the top of a hill, from where he saw smoke amongst the trees.

'I do not know what dangers are here,' he thought. 'I shall return to the ship to feast. Then I shall explore the island with my men.'

On his way back to the shore, Odysseus killed a stag and they feasted the whole of the day and night. At dawn, Odysseus divided his men into two groups: one led by him, the other by Eurylochus. After drawing lots, it was Eurylochus who set off first, taking twenty-two men with him.

Eurylochus did not return until dusk – and he was alone. He could hardly utter a word to his companions. At last, he spoke. 'We came to a beautiful house built of stone,' he wept. 'There were lions and wolves prowling around it, but they did not harm us. A woman was sitting in the porch, singing as she wove her tapestry. When she caught sight of us, she invited us to eat and drink with her. But I did not trust her. So I stood guard outside.'

'What happened?' Odysseus asked, his heart sinking. 'Where are the others?'

'The…the woman gave them cups of wine…then she

touched them with a wooden stick.' Eurylochus shuddered. 'They sprouted bristles and dropped to the ground. She had changed them into pigs! Then she laughed and drove them into a pigsty.'

Odysseus picked up his bow and sword. 'Come,' he said. 'We must go to that house and free them.'

'I cannot go with you!' Eurylochus wept.

'Then stay here and rest,' Odysseus replied. 'I shall go alone.'

As he made his way through the forest, Odysseus met Hermes, the messenger of the gods.

'Have you come to free your men from the enchantress, Circe?' he asked Odysseus. 'You must let me help, or you, too, will meet the same fate as them.' He stopped to pick a plant growing close by – a wild garlic. 'If you drink this, it will protect you from Circe's evil. When she has given you *her* magic potion, she will tap you with her stick. But her potion will have no power over you. At that same moment, you must draw your sword, as if you mean to kill her. She will beg forgiveness and you can ask her to undo the wrong she has done to your men.'

Odysseus did as Hermes instructed. And when he took his sword to threaten the enchantress, she was amazed. 'No man has ever resisted my magic powers,' she cried. 'Are you Odysseus? Hermes told me once that you would come this way from Troy!'

Circe commanded food and drink to be brought, and servants to wash Odysseus. But he shook his head. 'How can I accept what you offer when my men are still in your pigsty?' he asked.

Circe went at once to the pigsty and drove out the pigs. Then she smeared ointment on their backs. At once, they became men again, and they greeted Odysseus with tears of

joy. And Circe persuaded Odysseus to fetch his companions from the ship to rest and feast. Everybody came, except for Eurylochus. Odysseus would have slain him in anger, if the others had not prevented him. So he stayed behind to guard the ship.

The days passed in feasting and resting and they did not realise that a whole year had passed by. At last, Odysseus' companions persuaded him that it was time to sail on to Ithaca. He went to break the news to Circe.

'Leave, if that is what you wish,' Circe said. 'But I do not know the way to Ithaca. To find out how to get there, you must consult the prophet Tiresias. Only he has the knowledge that you need.'

'Where shall I find him?' Odysseus asked.

'In the Underworld,' Circe replied. 'In the Land of the Dead.'

Odysscus' heart almost broke at her words. 'Nobody has ever sailed a black ship into the Underworld and come back,' he said.

'Listen!' Circe replied. 'I shall tell you what to do when you get there.'

The men, thinking they were going home, prepared to sail – all except a young man called Elpenor, who was sleeping on the roof. As he hurried to join the others, he missed his footing and fell, breaking his neck.

When Odysseus told his men that they were going to the Underworld, they were heart-broken. But they sailed on, leaving their ship at the dark place where the two rivers of the dead flowed into one another.

CHAPTER THREE

Land of the Dead

'Dig a trench!' Odysseus commanded, 'and pour into it the milk and honey and wine that Circe has sent with us. We must pray to the ghosts of the dead below.'

When this had been done, Odysseus sacrificed the sheep that Circe had given them, and their blood ran into the trench, too. Now the souls of the dead came swarming towards them: young and old, warriors who had died in battle, still carrying their swords. Odysseus sat by the trench, sword drawn.

'Nobody must drink this blood until Tiresias comes,' he told himself.

The first spirit to approach him was one of his own men – the young Elpenor.

'What are you doing here in this land of shadows?' Odysseus asked him.

'You did not stop to bury me,' Elpenor replied. 'I beg you, master, before you sail home, to return to Circe's island and give me proper funeral rites. And on my grave, plant the oar that I used when I was alive.'

'I shall do as you ask, my poor Elpenor,' Odysseus replied.

Then, to his horror, Odysseus caught sight of his mother.

'She was alive when I set out for the Trojan War!' he thought, his eyes filling with tears. 'But I cannot allow her to approach until I have spoken to the prophet, Tiresias.'

At last, the blind Tiresias approached. Odysseus put his

sword away and let him pass by. When he had drunk blood, he spoke. 'Odysseus,' he said, 'Poseidon wishes to make your journey home difficult. He is still angry because you blinded his son, the Cyclops.'

'But how can we reach Ithaca safely?' Odysseus asked.

'Listen carefully,' Tiresias said. 'You will come to an island called Thrace, full of cattle and sheep which belong to the Sun god. If you kill any of them, you and your ship will be destroyed. Even if *you* manage to escape and come to Ithaca, you will find nothing but trouble. For there are men there courting your wife, Penelope. You *must* take your revenge on them.'

'If this is the will of the gods, so be it,' Odysseus replied. 'But tell me one more thing. The spirit of my dead mother is here. How can I make her recognise me?'

'Let her drink the blood and she will know you,' Tiresias replied.

Odysseus let his mother drink the sacrificed blood. At once, she gave a cry as she recognised her son. 'What are you doing here?' she wept.

'I have come to consult Tiresias,' he explained. 'But tell me what happened to you.'

'I died of grief because I thought you were dead,' his mother replied. 'Your wife is well and patient, although she weeps every day. And Telemachus is growing into a fine boy.'

'What about my father?' Odysseus asked. 'Does he keep order in Ithaca, in my place?'

'No,' his mother replied. 'He lives alone on his farm, in misery.'

As Odysseus reached out to embrace his mother, she slipped away from him. And more of the dead came towards Odysseus, among them King Agamemnon, who had led the Greeks to Troy, only to be killed by his wife's lover when he returned home. Then came Achilles, the greatest warrior of them all. Odysseus trembled with fear at the sight of so many dead.

'It is time to sail from these sad shores,' he commanded.

A soft west wind blew them back to Circe's island. Here they burned the body of Elpenor with full burial rites. After feasting together, Circe took Odysseus aside.

'I must warn you that many dangers still lie ahead of you,' she said. 'Listen, this is what you must do if you want to stay alive.'

CHAPTER FOUR

Danger at Sea

At dawn, Circe sent a favourable wind to take them on their way. But Odysseus was filled with fear at what Circe had told him.

'I must warn my men,' he thought. 'They must *all* know what to do when danger strikes.'

He called his men to him and told them what Circe had said. 'Soon we shall hear women's voices singing,' he said. 'These are the Sirens. They use their divine song to attract sailors to come too close. Then their ships are smashed against the rocks. You shall plug your ears with beeswax. But, I confess, I should like to hear their song. You must tie me to the mast and refuse to release me if I ask.'

Now their ship was approaching the island of the Sirens. The wind dropped and the men took up their oars to row. Odysseus cut pieces of wax to plug the ears of his men. Then he allowed them to tie him hand and foot to the ship's mast.

As they came closer, the Sirens broke into a high, clear song. 'Come and listen to our song, great Odysseus,' they sang.

Odysseus, longing to go closer, begged his men to free him. But they rowed on. As soon as they were safely past, they unplugged their ears and untied Odysseus.

And so they passed safely through the first danger.

But soon, they saw the waves raging ahead of them, throwing up sea spray like a cloud. Two enormous black rocks rose to the sky, leaving only a narrow sea-way for ships to pass through. Odysseus had not told his men about the horrors that lay there, for fear of making them panic.

'It is just as Circe described it,' Odysseus said to himself. 'To our left is the raging whirlpool, where the monster Charybdis sucks in the ships three times a day. To our right lives the monster Scylla. She has six heads, and in each are three mouths with three rows of grinding teeth. What can we do? We must pass through, even though these rocks can move and grind us to pieces.'

Then he called aloud, 'Oarsmen, strike the water hard! Men at the helm, steer the ship away from those foaming waves.'

In this way, they sailed up the narrow channel. But as they kept watch for Charybdis, Scylla snatched six men from the ship. She whisked them onto the rocks and devoured them as they screamed and stretched out their arms to Odysseus.

'I have never seen such a terrible sight,' he wept.

The men rowed as hard as they could, until at last, they reached the open sea. In front of them lay the island of Thrace, full of grazing cattle and sheep.

"If you kill any of them, you and your ship will be destroyed."

Odysseus told his men what the prophet Tiresias had said and commanded them to row on. But Eurylochus did not agree.

'We are *all* exhausted,' he said. 'Let us land on this shore for just one night, so that we may rest and eat the food that Circe gave us.'

The men cheered at his words.

'You force my hand, Eurylochus,' Odysseus said. 'But I ask every man to give me his solemn promise that he will not kill a single sheep or cow on that island.'

The men promised. They feasted on the shore and lay down to sleep. But, that night, Zeus sent a great storm, which raged for a whole month and they could not put their ship out to sea. Soon, their food was finished and they lived on fish and bird flesh.

Odysseus went to a sheltered place where he could pray to the gods. Then he fell into a deep sleep. When he awoke and set off for the ship, he could smell roasting meat.

'The gods lulled me to sleep while my men were planning this terrible crime!' he said to himself.

When he saw that his men had killed the cattle, Odysseus was angry.

'We would have starved,' Eurylochus said. 'And since we cannot undo what we have done, let us eat what we have killed.'

They feasted for six days, as the storm still raged around them. On the seventh day, the sun came out and the wind dropped.

'Let us hope that the Sun god has forgiven us,' Odysseus thought. 'Now we can set sail.'

But as soon as they had left the shore, a great wind blew up and ripped their sails. The mast split. A bolt of lightning struck the ship and everybody was thrown into the sea. Odysseus' men floated like seagulls on the waves. Then, one by one, they sank beneath the water.

'There will be no homecoming for them,' Odysseus wept.

He tied himself to the mast of his ship, which had now toppled into the sea. To his horror, the sea washed him back towards Scylla's rock. As Charybdis was beginning to suck him into the whirlpool, he managed to catch hold of a fig tree and held on grimly until the mast was washed up.

'Thank the gods that Scylla did not catch sight of me,' Odysseus thought. 'Nothing could have saved me then.'

Clinging to the mast, Odysseus drifted for nine days, more dead than alive. At last, he was washed up on the shore of a distant island, where no ships ever sailed.

'How will I ever get home to Ithaca now?' Odysseus wept.

CHAPTER FIVE

The Island of Calypso

It was the nymph Calypso who found Odysseus. She fell in love with him and offered to make him immortal, but he refused. Seven years passed by. And as Odysseus sat pining on that sad shore, his son, Telemachus, was growing into manhood.

Athene put on her golden sandals, seized her bronze spear and sped to Ithaca – to Odysseus' palace, where she disguised herself as a family friend. She found the palace full of young men, who had come to ask for Penelope's hand in marriage. They had slaughtered cattle and were drinking and eating everything in sight.

'These men are living off a man whose bones may be rotting in a distant land,' Telemachus whispered. 'Who are you? What has brought you here?'

'I know that Odysseus is alive and he will think of a way to come back to you,' Athene said. She stared at Telemachus. 'Your likeness to your father is startling!'

'If only he would return!' Telemachus cried. 'My mother does not want to remarry, and these suitors are eating us out of house and home.'

'Tell them to leave,' Athene said. 'And take your best men and ship and go to King Nestor and King Menelaus. Your father fought with them at Troy. They may have news of him.'

When the stranger had left, Telemachus was filled with the courage to plan such a journey. At last, he set sail.

But the misfortune of Odysseus weighed heavily on Athene's heart and she spoke of it to her father, Zeus. He called the gods to a meeting, all except Poseidon, who had gone to visit the eastern shores of Africa.

'Look how Odysseus sits in misery on that island,' Athene said. 'He has no ship to carry him home to his beloved Ithaca. And I fear the suitors may murder Telemachus on his way back.'

'Yes, it is time for Odysseus to return home,' Zeus said. He called his messenger, Hermes, to his side. 'Go and tell Calypso what we have decided,' he said. 'And you, Athene, do what you can for Telemachus.'

Hermes quickly put on his golden sandals that carried him with the speed of wind. He picked up the wand with which he could cast a spell. Then he swooped over the sea and skimmed the waves like a seagull. At last, he came to the cave where Calypso was living.

A large fire was blazing in the hearth. Calypso was singing with her beautiful voice as she wove her fine cloths. Grapes hung above her, and spring water ran by. It was a beautiful place. But Odysseus was sitting on the shore, weeping as he looked across the sea, tormented by thoughts of home.

Calypso recognised Hermes. 'What brings *you* all this way?' she asked. 'You are a welcome guest. I shall gladly do as you ask.'

'Zeus has sent me,' Hermes replied. 'He has told me that you have here a man dogged by bad luck, who has fought in Troy for nine years, has lost all his companions and wishes to return home. You must send him to Ithaca without delay. The gods wish him to see his friends and family once more.'

'You gods are hard-hearted,' Calypso said. 'You do not

like me to be with a mortal man, a man I rescued from death. But if that is Zeus' wish, let him go.'

Hermes thanked her and left at once. Calypso went to Odysseus, where he sat weeping. 'My unhappy friend, do not weep any longer,' she said. 'Come now; chop down some trees to make a raft. I shall give you food and water – and a fine wind so that you may reach your country safe and sound.'

Odysseus shuddered. 'I cannot cross such a sea on a raft, unless I have your promise that no harm will come to me,' he said.

Calypso smiled and stroked his hand. 'How can you say such a thing, Odysseus! I swear by the gods above that I shall not plot against you. I wish you happiness. But if you knew the misery you will meet on your way, you would stay – however much you long to see your wife again.'

'My dear wife, Penelope, cannot compare to you, Calypso. She is only a human, not a goddess. But I want to go home. I have seen many disasters these last years. One more will not matter.'

When dawn came, Calypso put on a silver dress with a golden belt. She gave Odysseus a great bronze axe and showed him where the best trees grew. And so his work began. By the end of the fourth day, the raft was ready. Calypso provided Odysseus with fine clothes, water and wine and sacks of grain and meat. Then she commanded a warm, soft breeze.

'Keep the star of Orion the Hunter always to your left as you sail,' she told him.

With a happy heart, Odysseus spread his sail to catch the wind. He never closed his eyes, not once, but watched Orion all the time. In this way, he sailed for seventeen days.

On the eighteenth day, he caught his first glimpse of land – the shadowy mountains of the country of the Phaeacians. It was here that Poseidon spotted him as he returned from Africa.

'So Zeus has helped Odysseus while I was away!' he said to himself.

Poseidon stirred up the sea, and covered the land and sea with cloud. He whipped up great waves that terrified Odysseus.

'What will become of me?' he asked himself. 'Calypso was right. There is great misery for me before I reach home.'

As the sea tossed the raft backwards and forwards, Odysseus was thrown into the water. Only a goddess in the shape of a seagull saved him.

'Take off your heavy clothes and swim to shore,' she said. 'Wrap my veil around your wrist to keep you from harm.'

Odysseus did as the goddess said and set out for the shore. But he would have been crushed against the rocks if he had not held on to a spur of rock. Then he managed to swim to calmer waters.

There he threw the veil back into the sea and staggered inland, following the bank of a river. Then, feeling his strength drain away, he crept under an olive tree, covered himself with their leaves and slept at last.

CHAPTER SIX

Help at Last

Odysseus had been washed up in the land of the
Phaeacians, a country ruled by the mighty King Alcinous.
He had a young daughter called Nausica. As she lay
sleeping, Athene whispered in her ear, 'Nausica, every man
in this land wants you for his wife, but you are so lazy!
Look at all your dirty clothes! Go down to the river and
wash them.'

At dawn, Nausica told her mother and father about her
dream, and they let her take a wagon and servants to the
river. Here, they washed and feasted and bathed. And here,
Athene woke up Odysseus. He crept out from the olive
bush and made his way towards the young women. He was
not a pleasant sight: dirty and grimy with salt. Everybody
ran away, except Nausica.

'Princess, how beautiful you are!' Odysseus said,
kneeling at her feet. 'I have been washed up on your shore
and I know no one in this country. Give me rags to wrap
myself in so that I can go to the nearest town.'

'Sir,' she replied. 'I know from the way you speak that
you are a good man. I am the daughter of the great
Alcinous. I can take you to him.'

Odysseus bathed in the river and put on clean clothes
that the servants brought him. Nausica stared at him in
admiration.

'There will be gossip if I return with this handsome
stranger,' she said to herself. 'I shall go first. Then he can

follow me.'

When it was time for Odysseus to set off, Athene wrapped him in a thick mist. As he walked, he marvelled at the harbours full of ships and at the high city walls. Soon Odysseus approached the king's palace. Its golden doors, guarded on each side by silver dogs, revealed a hall where the chieftains held their meetings. Golden statues of young boys held out flaming torches. Within the bronze walls of the palace lay a large orchard, full of trees which bore fruit all through the year.

Odysseus, full of admiration, wondered at it all. Then he stepped inside. Still covered in mist, he threw his arms around the queen's knees. As the mist rolled away, silence fell.

'I come to beg for your husband's help,' Odysseus cried. 'I have lived through many hardships and wish only for you to return me to my own country.'

The wise king, advised by his elders, raised Odysseus to his feet and gave him food and wine. 'We shall help you, friend, unless you turn out to be one of the gods playing a trick on us.'

'Do not fear, I am a human being,' Odysseus replied. 'I have had hard times indeed. I want only to see my wife and family before I die.'

When everybody had left for their own homes, the queen, recognising the clothes he was wearing, asked, 'Where do you come from? Who gave you those clothes?'

'Your Majesty, I shall not bore you with all my troubles,' Odysseus replied, 'for the gods have sent me so many. Bad luck took me to the island of Calypso. No god or human ever goes to her island. She took me in and looked after me. But she never won my heart. I stayed seven years, until her change of heart – or Zeus himself –

allowed me to leave. Poseidon stirred the sea and winds against me. I was washed ashore here and I asked your daughter for help.'

'Then she should have brought you home herself,' the king said, 'for she was the one you asked for help.'

'Do not blame her, sir.'

'My friend,' the king went on, 'I wish that a man like you would stay here and marry her. But we would not detain you if you wish to go. And to put your mind at rest, let us fix the day of your departure: tomorrow.'

Odysseus' patient heart was filled with happiness that night as he prayed, 'O Father Zeus, grant that Alcinous may carry out his promise and that I shall now return to the land of my fathers.'

And at last, Odysseus lay down to sleep, knowing that the very next day, he would sail home to Ithaca.

CHAPTER SEVEN

The Games!

As soon as dawn appeared, the mighty Alcinous led Odysseus to the place by the ships where the Phaeacians held their meetings. Here they sat, side by side, on seats of polished marble. In a short time, many people gathered to see the stranger.

'Captains and counsellors of the Phaeacians,' the king said, 'this stranger has come to ask for help, and I have granted it. Take a ship down to the sea and pick fifty-two oarsmen. Then come inside to eat with us before you sail.'

Alcinous led Odysseus to the great hall of the palace, where his servants sacrificed to the gods a dozen sheep, eight boars and two oxen. A minstrel sang and played his lute as they feasted, and Odysseus pulled his purple cloak across his face to hide his tears. The king noticed his distress and stood up to speak.

'Phaeacians!' he shouted. 'We have eaten our fill and listened to the lute. Now let us go outside and show our skill at sport. When our guest reaches his home, he can tell his friends of our great skill in boxing, wrestling and jumping.'

With these words, he led the way outside. There was no lack of fine men to compete that day, including the three sons of Alcinous. The first event was a race. The contestants ran at full speed from the start, raising a cloud of dust on the track. The wrestling match was won by a young man called Euryalus. Other sports followed: the jump, boxing – and throwing the discus.

When they had all enjoyed these sports, one of the king's sons rose to his feet and called, 'Friends! Let us see if our visitor is an expert at sport. He is well-built, with strong arms and legs. He is not old, only weakened by hardship. There is nothing like the sea to break a man, however strong he is.' He turned to Odysseus. 'Come, sir. Your ship is ready. Won't you take part in our games before you sail?'

'I am too sick at heart to think of games,' Odysseus replied. 'All I want to do is go home.'

'You are quite right, sir!' Euryalus cried. 'I did not think you were an athlete!'

Odysseus glared at him, angered by this insult. 'You are a fool, and your words have angered me. In spite of what I have been through, I shall try my hand at your sports.'

With these words, Odysseus leapt to his feet. Without taking off his cloak, he picked up the biggest discus of all. With one swing, he hurled it. Everybody cowered as it flew above their heads. It landed further away than any of the other throws.

'Now, can you do better than that?' he asked the young men around him. 'Or would you like to take me on at boxing, wrestling or even running? Who will challenge me? I am ready to match myself against any of you.' He paused. 'I am good at all sport, but I handle the bow best. I was one of the best archers at Troy.'

When he had finished speaking, the crowds stood silent.

'My friend,' the king said at last, 'we accept what you say. You were angry at being insulted in this way. We are good at sport. But what we like best is feasting and music and dancing. So come and watch our best dancers.'

When Odysseus had marvelled at the beauty of the

dancing, the king called for the princes of his kingdom to bring gifts for Odysseus. And he called for Euryalus to apologise.

'I shall do as you ask, Lord Alcinous,' he replied. 'Here is my gift: a bronze sword with a silver hilt.' He handed the sword to Odysseus. 'Honoured guest, I salute you,' he said, 'may the wind blow away the offensive words that came from my lips. And may you return home in safety.'

As they feasted for the last time together, Odysseus asked the minstrel, 'Before I set sail, will you sing about the wooden horse for us?'

The minstrel did as he asked. And as he sang, Odysseus' heart melted with grief and tears ran from his eyes. He wept as a woman weeps when her husband has fallen in battle. The King saw his tears and ordered the minstrel to stop playing.

'Now, sir,' he said to Odysseus, 'tell me your name. Tell me which city you come from. Tell us what sorrow makes you weep as you listen to the fall of Troy. Did you lose many companions to the Trojan spears?'

'I am Odysseus,' he replied, 'and I am the only man left from twelve ships that I took to Troy.'

Everybody in the hall gasped, because they all knew his name. And, far into that night, he told them of his journey so far: of the Cyclops, of Circe, of the Land of the Dead, of Scylla and Charybdis, how he lost his ships and men – and how he had come from Calypso.

When his tale was finished, everybody sat in silence in that shadowy hall, held in the spell of his words. Then, as dawn approached, preparations were made to set sail. Odysseus wrapped himself in warm rugs and lay on the deck to sleep. The oarsmen swung back and untied the rope that held them to the shore.

And like a horse jumping at the lash of the whip, the ship leapt into the water and sped through the waves to Ithaca.

CHAPTER EIGHT

Home Again

When Odysseus awoke, he was lying under an olive tree, where the Phaeacians had placed him. Athene had shrouded him in a thick mist.

'I do not want anybody to recognise Odysseus,' she thought, 'not until he has had his revenge on all Penelope's suitors.'

But Odysseus did not recognise his own country. 'Where have I landed this time?' he cried. 'Why have the Phaeacians brought me to this terrible dark place?'

Athene, disguised as a young shepherd, told him that he had come to Ithaca. Then she revealed herself. '*I* have brought you here,' she said, 'and protected you along the way. But you must now be patient. Do not tell anybody that you have returned from your wanderings. Suffer everything in silence, even the worst insults.'

'Am I really back in my beloved land?' he asked.

Athene dispersed the mist and joy came, at last, to the long-suffering Odysseus. She bade him to hide the gifts he had brought back. Then she sat down next to him.

'Odysseus,' she said, 'Penelope has pined all these years for you. Suitors have been pestering her these last three years, and offering her marriage gifts. They would certainly have killed you if you had suddenly appeared. And Telemachus has gone to seek news of you.'

'Tell me what to do!' Odysseus cried.

'I am going to change the way you look,' Athene

replied. 'I shall wither your skin, turn your dark hair grey and clothe you in rags. Then you must go to your swineherd, Eumaeus. He will be loyal to you. Wait there until I bring Telemachus home safely.'

As soon as she had gone, Odysseus left the harbour, and tracked through the woods until he came to the swineherd, the most worthy of all his servants. He made Odysseus welcome, and talked of his master.

'He's dead, I am certain of it,' he said sadly.

'My friend,' Odysseus said. 'Odysseus is coming back, I swear it. And he will punish all those who dishonour his wife.'

As they feasted on roast pork, Odysseus amused him with tales he had heard of the Trojan War until it was time to sleep.

And all this time, Athene was urging Telemachus to return home to Ithaca.

'Sail at night,' she told him, 'for the suitors plan to ambush you on the way. And go straight to Eumaeus, not to your mother.'

Odysseus and Eumaeus were preparing their breakfast in the dawn light, when a young man came through the farm gate.

'This must be my son!' Odysseus thought, 'for he looks so much like me.'

When they had all eaten together, Telemachus said, 'Eumaeus, go to my mother and tell her that I have returned safely. Do not tell anybody else, for I trust nobody. Then come straight back here.'

As soon as Eumaeus had left, Athene whispered in Odysseus' ear, 'Tell him who you are, *now*!' She touched Odysseus with her golden wand. She gave him back his

youth. His cheeks were smooth, his beard and hair were black again. And he wore a fresh cloak and tunic.

'Stranger,' Telemachus said. 'You are not the same as before. Are you a god?'

'No, I am your father,' Odysseus said, tears running down his cheeks. He kissed his son.

'No, it is not true!' Telemachus cried. 'You are playing a trick on me.'

'It *is* me!' Odysseus said again. 'With the help of Athene, I am back in my own land after twenty years of wandering.'

Telemachus flung his arms around his father's neck and burst into tears.

'Now it is time to rid ourselves of your mother's suitors,' Odysseus said.

'Father, I know you are a great fighter,' his son cried, 'but there are more than eighty of them!'

'Let us hope that Athene and Zeus will be all the help we need,' his father replied. 'Listen, my son! You must go home to those arrogant suitors. Show no anger at the way they will treat me when I appear. And when I give the signal, hide all the weapons that are in the great hall. Tell *nobody* that you have seen me.'

And in the harbour of Ithaca, Antinous – the leader of the suitors – saw that Telemachus' ship had come back safely.

'The gods have saved him from certain death,' he cursed.

CHAPTER NINE

The Beggar and the Bow

Odysseus, having sent Telemachus on ahead, now prepared to go to his palace with Eumaeus. Dressed as a wretched beggar in filthy rags, he hobbled along, leaning on a wooden stick. Soon they came to his palace and heard music and the sound of feasting. Telemachus gave him a bowl and told him to beg from each of his mother's suitors.

Odysseus approached Antinous. 'Give me something, my friend,' he begged. 'You seem the noblest of the lords here and should give me more than the others. I was once one of the lucky ones and lived in a palace like this.'

'What god has inflicted this man on us?' Antinous cried. 'He is spoiling my meal! Keep away from my table.'

He picked up a stool and struck Odysseus' right shoulder, but he did not flinch. The other suitors scolded Antinous for what he had done, but he took no notice. Penelope was angry, too, and sent for the stranger.

'That beggar has the look of a man who has travelled far,' she thought, 'and he may have news of my husband.'

At sunset, when they were alone at last by the fire in the great hall, Penelope asked, 'Stranger, who are you? Where have you come from?'

'I am a man of many sorrows,' Odysseus replied.

'Sir, I, too am alone in my misery,' she replied, 'ever since my husband sailed to Troy. I long for Odysseus. My suitors are now forcing me to name a wedding day. I have put them off for three years by weaving a tapestry – a shroud for Odysseus' father. I refused to marry until it was finished. But each night, I unpicked what I had woven during the day. Yes, I deceived them, until I was found out.'

'My lady,' Odysseus said. 'Do not weep any longer for your husband. I have news of him. He is close by, on his way home with a large fortune.'

'May this prove to be true!' Penelope said, 'although I have heard it many times. Now let me bring Odysseus' old nurse to wash your feet.'

The old woman began her work at once. 'You remind me very strongly of my master,' she said. Then she touched the scar on his foot, the one made by the tusk of a boar when he was a child. 'You *are* Odysseus!' she cried.

'Do not let anybody learn the truth,' Odysseus whispered.

The next day, Penelope came into the hall carrying Odysseus' shining bow made of horn.

'Come now, my brave lords!' she cried to the suitors. 'Your reward now stands before you. The suitor who can shoot an arrow through the rings of twelve axe handles, shall claim me as his bride.'

The target was set up and each man failed in turn. Odysseus appeared in the doorway and asked to be allowed to test his strength and skill. The lords laughed, but Penelope told him come forward.

'And shall you marry a beggar?' one of the suitors cried.

Amidst loud jeering, Odysseus bent back the bow – and his arrow sped through each ring.

'I have done no dishonour to your father's bow,' he said to Telemachus. 'But now it is time *we* hunted and made the kill,' he whispered.

And Odysseus, throwing off his ragged clothes, stood in

the doorway of the great hall.

'My Lords, the contest that was to decide your fate is now over!' he shouted.

Odysseus aimed his great bow at Antinous, who was just about to take a sip of wine. An arrow passed right through his neck and he fell to the floor – dead.

CHAPTER TEN

The Final Battle

There was uproar in the hall. The other suitors searched the walls for armour, but not a shield or sword was hanging there. They turned on Odysseus. 'Now you will die, stranger!' they cried. 'You have killed the greatest nobleman in Ithaca.'

'You dogs!' Odysseus shouted. 'You stole from my household behind my back. You pestered my wife. You never thought you would see her husband return from Troy!'

At his words, fear drained the colour from their cheeks. At last, one of them, a suitor called Eurymachus, spoke. 'Antinous was the chief culprit and now he lies dead,' he said. 'So spare the rest of us.'

'Nothing will stop me from killing you all,' Odysseus replied. 'Face me and fight.'

Eurymachus drew his two-edged sword and leapt at Odysseus with a blood-curdling shout. At the same moment, Odysseus let an arrow fly, piercing his breast. Others came to fight him, and Telemachus went to bring more weapons. But the goatherd, loyal to the suitors and not to Odysseus, knew a secret way to the room where the armour was stored and he fetched weapons for them. Seeing the suitors armed in this way, Odysseus trembled.

'Where is your courage, Odysseus?' Athene asked. 'You fought against the Trojans for ten years! Yet now, in your own home, you tremble.'

And when the suitors threw their spears together, they all missed – thanks to Athene. But Odysseus and his helpers found their mark every time. And, at last, they drew their swords and charged. The suitors ran like a herd of cattle stampeding. And they were all slain, piled in the hall like fish on a seashore.

The old nurse found the blood-spattered Odysseus sitting amongst the corpses like a lion dripping blood from his jaw.

'Bring my wife to me!' he commanded.

As he waited, people in the royal palace flocked to him, to embrace him in welcome.

Penelope, who had been sleeping deeply, made her way to the hall and sat down in the firelight. But she still did not recognise Odysseus because of the vile clothes he was wearing. Telemachus scolded her.

'My child,' she said, 'I still cannot be sure.'

Patient Odysseus called Telemachus to him. 'We must not forget that we have killed the finest of Ithaca's men, and their families will surely seek revenge. Let us put on fresh clothes and feast, so that passers-by think this is a wedding-feast. This will stop the news of slaughter spreading through the town for the time being. Then I must visit our country estate and my father, and decide what is to be done.'

The servants washed Odysseus until he looked as handsome as a god.

'Make up my bed in a corner of the hall,' he called to the servants, 'for tonight I must sleep alone.'

Penelope knew at once how she could test her husband. She ordered their bridal bed to be brought out into the hall.

Odysseus smiled. 'That is not possible!' he said. 'I built that bed myself. Its corner posts are rooted olive trees,

which nobody can move.'

Penelope's heart melted. She threw her arms around her husband and kissed him. 'Do not be angry,' she said, 'for all these twenty years, I have feared that somebody would come and deceive me.'

Odysseus kissed her, and told her of his wanderings after leaving Troy – telling her, too, that another journey lay before him.

'The prophet Tiresias told me that I must travel over land, carrying an oar,' he said. 'And when I come to the right place, I must plant my oar in the earth and make sacrifices to Poseidon. Only then shall I be free of his anger.

At dawn, Odysseus set off to see his old father, Laertes. He found him alone in the vineyard, shabby and dirty and full of grief. Odysseus embraced him and showed him the tusk scar on his foot.

The old man threw his arms around his beloved son and they talked and feasted. As news of Odysseus' return and the slaughter of Penelope's suitors reached everybody's ears, their families gathered outside the palace. Antinous' father called for revenge. They ran for their weapons and set off for Laertes' farm. As their spears glinted in the sunlight, Odysseus went forward to meet them.

'Men of Ithaca!' Athene cried. 'Do not spill any more blood.'

At Athene's cry, the men who had come to fight panicked and took flight. Odysseus ran after them, and would have fought on, if Zeus had not thrown a thunderbolt at his feet.

'Odysseus!' Athene cried. 'Do not fight your fellow-men, or you will face the wrath of Zeus.'

At her words, the anger died down in Odysseus.

And in this way, peace came to Ithaca – and to Odysseus himself.